Cinderella

❧ Fairy Tale Treasury ❧

Adapted by
Jane Jerrard

Illustrated by
Susan Spellman

Publications International, Ltd.

Once upon a time, there was a young girl who was sweet, kind, and pretty. But she had a very mean stepmother who made her life a misery. The stepmother and her two daughters made the girl do all the work of the house. They called the girl "Cinderella" because at night she would sit among the cinders on the hearth and warm herself.

Cinderella was always cheerful, even though she had to work very hard.

One exciting day, an invitation to the Prince's fancy ball arrived! All the fine people in the land were invited, and the sisters worried about what to wear and how to behave with a prince.

Poor Cinderella sewed and ironed for days, but she herself was not going to the ball. She was only a servant, after all. Besides, she did not have a gown to wear.

As the stepmother and her daughters rode off to the ball, Cinderella ran to the garden and cried. Suddenly, a beautiful woman magically appeared. She was Cinderella's Fairy Godmother!

"What is the matter, Cinderella?" asked the Fairy Godmother.

Cinderella explained that she wanted very much to go to the ball and see the Prince.

So, with a wave of her magic wand, Cinderella's Fairy Godmother turned a pumpkin into a beautiful coach. Then she turned six mice into fine gray horses, and a fat white rat into a coachman!

And with one touch of her wand, the Fairy Godmother turned Cinderella's old dress into a lovely gown trimmed in gold and silver. Best of all, she gave the girl a pair of tiny glass slippers that fit just right!

As Cinderella stepped into the waiting coach, her Fairy Godmother warned, "You must be home by midnight, Cinderella, because all my magic will disappear when the clock strikes twelve!"

Cinderella promised she would not be late, and off she went to the ball, her heart pounding with excitement.

The Prince was quite taken with beautiful Cinderella. In fact, everyone at the ball loved her! As the Prince and Cinderella danced, all the people smiled and watched.

The Prince asked Cinderella to dance every dance that night. Cinderella was so happy she forgot the time. As the clock began to strike twelve, she ran from the palace. She was in such a hurry that she lost one of the glass slippers!

Cinderella had to run all the way home in her rags that night, for her coach was now a pumpkin again, and the mice and the rat had run away. All that was left of her beautiful outfit was the other glass slipper.

The Prince ran after Cinderella. He wanted to call out to her, but he realized that she had never told him her name! When he found the glass slipper on the palace steps, the Prince vowed to find its owner.

The next day, the Prince was very unhappy. He had fallen in love with the girl without a name. He decided at once to search the land for the woman who could wear the glass slipper.

The prince and his servants went to every house, inviting each woman to try on the little shoe—but not one foot could fit into it!

At last, his carriage arrived at Cinderella's house.

The stepsisters tried, but they could not squeeze into the tiny shoe. When Cinderella asked to try, the Prince knelt and slipped the shoe easily onto her little foot. Cinderella had carefully kept the other glass slipper. Now she pulled it from her apron pocket and put it on, too.

All of the sudden, Cinderella was magically dressed in a beautiful gown. The Prince took Cinderella back to the palace and they were married that very day!